Wedding in Delhi

Contents

Chapter 1

The Invitation

Jasmine was a worrier. She worried about getting sunburnt in summer and frostbite in winter, she worried about meeting new people and trying new things.

Then one day Jasmine's mum rushed into her bedroom holding a card. "Guess what?" she cried. "Your cousin Dev is getting married and we're all invited to the wedding. We're going to Delhi!"

Wedding
in Delhi

by Katie Dale and Amit Tayal

W

FRANKLIN WATTS

Jasmine's eyes widened. She had always wanted to visit her cousins Priti and Dev, and India sounded like an amazing country.

But Jasmine was nervous. "I've n-never been on a p-plane before," she stammered. "It's scary. And what if I get travel sick?"

"You'll be fine!" her mum laughed. "Jasmine, you worry too much! This adventure will be good for you."

Jasmine's mum took her shopping for a lovely new outfit. Jasmine twirled happily. She couldn't wait to go the wedding – she'd never been to one before. But then they had to get travel jabs.
"All done," the nurse said.
"That didn't hurt at all!" Jasmine cried, relieved.

At last it was time to fly to Delhi. Jasmine clutched her seat nervously as the engine started. Jasmine's tummy fluttered as the plane rumbled across the runway, faster and faster. She held her breath and squeezed her eyes closed ... then suddenly everything went quiet. Jasmine opened one eye and peeked out of the window.

The plane was soaring smoothly through the sky. It was amazing!

"The cars look as small as ants," Jasmine gasped, watching them shrink beneath her as the plane rose higher and higher.

Soon they were far above the puffy white clouds. Jasmine beamed. It was beautiful. Better still,

she didn't get travel sick. She watched a couple of films, ate a meal on a little tray, then fell fast asleep.

Chapter 2

In India

When Jasmine woke up, they were in India.
In the airport, a girl Jasmine's age raced towards
them followed by her parents.

"You must be
Jasmine!" she cried.
"I recognise you
from the photos."
"Yes," Jasmine said
shyly. "You must be
Priti." Priti nodded
happily. "Welcome
to Delhi!"

Outside, the sun was shining and the heat hit Jasmine like a wave. "What if I get sunburnt?" she fretted. "Don't worry," said her mum. "We've got extra-strong sun cream."

As they drove to Priti's house, traffic filled the roads and horns blared everywhere. Jasmine gazed out of the window in wonder. There were cars, motorbikes with three or four people clinging on and things that looked like a cross between a car and a motorbike. Then suddenly Jasmine's jaw dropped.

"Look out!" she cried. "There's a cow crossing the road!"

"Don't worry," Priti laughed as the cars neatly avoided the animal. "There are cows everywhere here."

"Wow," Jasmine gasped. "That's incredible."

Soon, they arrived at Priti's house.

It was decorated with flowers and lights.

"Welcome, Jasmine," Dev greeted his cousin.

Jasmine's jaw dropped. His skin was yellow!

"Oh no," she gasped. "Are you ill, Dev?"

"No, don't worry," Dev laughed. "It's just turmeric paste – for good luck." Jasmine smiled. What a relief.

"Come and join in," Priti said, grinning as she scooped up a handful of yellow paste. Dev laughed as everyone coated him in paste.

"Savita can't wait to meet you, Jasmine," Dev said. "You'll meet her at the Sangeet party tonight. Nearly everybody who's going to the wedding will be there." Jasmine gulped. That sounded like a lot of strangers she would have to meet.

The Sangeet party was enormous. Jasmine's jaw dropped as she stepped inside. Everyone was dressed in vibrant colours and sparkly jewellery, and every room was decorated with brightly coloured cloth, cushions and decorations. It was beautiful. They found Savita sitting on a colourful cushion as a girl squeezed dark brown paste onto her arm.

"Welcome!" Savita greeted them. "Would you like a henna tattoo? Everyone's getting them done for the wedding."

"Do I have to?" Jasmine asked anxiously. She'd seen people with them in England but had always been wary of trying it herself.

"Don't worry, it's not a real tattoo," Priti said. "It's just plant dye. When it dries and peels off you'll have a lovely pattern on your skin."

"Would you like to get one, Jasmine?"

her mum asked. "I am going to have one."

Jasmine bit her lip. A henna tattoo couldn't be bad

if her mum was getting one, could it?

"You don't have to," Savita said kindly. "And if you

don't like it, don't worry. It'll fade away in a few days."

Jasmine took a deep breath and nodded.

"Okay, I'll get one." She chose a pattern and the girl

painted beautiful flowers and swirls down her arm.

"It's so pretty!" Jasmine cried happily.

Then a lady came round giving out bangles

and Jasmine chose some that would match

her blue outfit perfectly.

"Come on, it's time for the dancing," Priti cried, jumping up. She led Jasmine to another room where lots of Savita's relatives took it in turns to perform dances while everyone watched and clapped. Jasmine clapped along happily. Each dance was so different and wonderful.

"I'm thirsty," Priti said. "Wait here, I'll get us a drink."

Suddenly even louder music started and now everyone hurried onto the dance floor. Jasmine's cheeks grew hot. She looked around but Priti had disappeared into the crowd. She couldn't see Dev or Savita or her parents anywhere. She didn't know anyone, and she felt very shy among so many strangers. She huddled in a corner out of the way.

"There you are, Jasmine," Priti said, returning with two cups. "Come and dance!"

Jasmine bit her lip. She loved dancing but she didn't want to look silly in front of so many strangers.

"I can't," she confessed. "I don't know any of these people."

"That doesn't matter," Priti laughed, putting the cups down and tugging Jasmine onto the dance floor, "I don't know most of them either."

Jasmine smiled. Soon everyone was dancing and laughing together. It was great fun!

Chapter 3

Wedding Day

When Jasmine awoke in the morning, she realised
it was the wedding day. She put on her new outift
and bangles and anxiously checked her reflection.

"Are you ready?" Priti asked, bounding in.

"Do I look okay?" Jasmine asked.

"You look perfect!" Priti said. "Come on,

it's time for the Baraat."

"What's that?" Jasmine asked.

"I'll show you. Follow me!" Priti grinned,

leading her outside.

There was a huge crowd of family and

musicians waiting in front of the house.

"We're all going to dance and sing all the way to the wedding in a huge procession with Dev," Priti said.

"How wonderful," Jasmine beamed, searching the colourful crowd. "But where is Dev?"

Priti pointed and Jasmine gasped. Dev was riding a big decorated white horse.

"What if he falls off and hurts himself?"
Jasmine cried.

"Oh, Jasmine," Priti laughed. "You worry too much. Let your hair down and have fun!" She pulled Jasmine's hair out of its ponytail and grinned.

Jasmine smiled. It was hard not to have fun as they all danced and sang through the streets. Everyone they passed smiled and waved and cheered. It was like a carnival.

When they arrived at the wedding venue, Savita's family greeted them. Everyone took their seats and Jasmine watched nervously as Dev took off his shoes and walked towards a big fire. She hoped he didn't get burned.

Suddenly everyone turned. Savita had arrived.

She looked absolutely beautiful dressed in lots of sparkly jewellery and a deep red dress. As Savita reached Dev she put a flower garland around his neck. Then Dev put a garland around her neck.

"I hope neither of them get hayfever," said Jasmine.

"Oh, Jasmine," Priti giggled.

Dev looked over at Priti and raised an eyebrow.

"Oops, I nearly forgot my job!" Priti hissed, jumping up and hurrying to the front. She carefully picked up the end of Dev's scarf and Savita's saree and tied them together. Dev and Savita held hands and beamed at her.

"The knot represents their eternal bond," Priti said as she hurried back to her seat. "Good thing I didn't forget to tie it!"

Holding hands, Dev and Savita walked around the fire several times. Jasmine crossed her fingers anxiously, but luckily neither of them got burned. As Savita and Dev finished circling the fire they rushed to sit down. Their families laughed.

"What's so funny?" Jasmine asked.

"It is said whoever sits down first will rule the house," Priti explained, giggling.

Jasmine smiled. It looked like Savita was going to be the boss in that house!

Next, a boy laid out seven stones on the floor, and Savita and Dev touched each one with their toes.

"What are they doing now?" Jasmine whispered.

"Each step is a prayer," Priti replied. "For food, strength, prosperity, wisdom, children, health and friendship."

When they sat back down, Savita swapped seats and sat on Dev's left side.

"It's so she can be as close as possible to his heart," Priti said.

"How romantic," Jasmine sighed.

Dev placed a necklace of black and gold beads around Savita's neck, and dabbed red powder on her forehead. Finally, they exchanged rings and everybody clapped. They looked so happy.

"They're officially married," Priti cried.

"Hurray!" Jasmine clapped. Then she frowned. "Oh no. Look!"

Two little girls were stealing Dev's shoes. "Stop!" Jasmine ran after them. She couldn't let them spoil Savita and Dev's wedding. Not after they'd survived the horse and the flowers and the fire.

Chapter 4

Missing Shoes

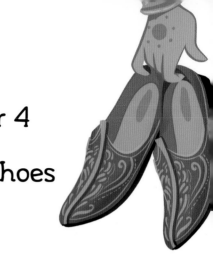

Jasmine found the little girls giggling in a corner.

"What are you doing with Dev's shoes?" she asked.

"Give them back."

The little girls looked up at her, wide-eyed.

"Don't worry," Priti laughed, catching up with

Jasmine. "It's all part of the fun,"

"What do you mean?" Jasmine asked, frowning.

"You'll see," Priti said, smiling as she turned

to the girls. "Come on, let's find Dev."

"We've got your shoes, Dev!" the little girls cried, running up to him. Dev laughed. He gave them some coins and sweets and they put his shoes back on his feet.

"It's a tradition," Priti explained to Jasmine. "The bride's sisters sometimes steal the groom's shoes at weddings." Jasmine smiled, relieved that everything was okay. Her mum and Priti were right. She really should relax more.

"Congratulations," she told Savita and Dev.

"Thank you so much for coming to share our special day," Dev said.

"I've enjoyed it," Jasmine smiled. "It was all so fascinating."

"Your henna looks beautiful," Savita added, smiling.

"Thank you," Jasmine said, beaming. "I'm so glad I got it done."

"Dinner time!" Priti cried. Jasmine stared at the array of different dishes laid out on the tables. There was so much food. There were all sorts of curries, rice, pastries, and so many chutneys she didn't recognise. Jasmine bit her lip and picked out a few bhajis. She knew she liked bhajis.

"Aren't you hungry?" asked Priti, loading her plate.

"Yes, but I've never tried most of this food and there aren't any labels," Jasmine said. "What if I don't like it?"

"You'll never know unless you try," Priti laughed.

Jasmine thought about the jabs and the plane journey and henna tattoos and dancing and all the things she'd been nervous about. They'd all turned out fine. More than fine. She'd had a great time.

"You're right, Priti," Jasmine said. "I'll never know what I like unless I try." She picked up a plate and took a little bit of each dish to taste. To her surprise, she liked nearly everything. She eagerly went back for more food and filled her plate.

"Save room for the sweets," Priti warned.

After dinner it was time for the party! This time Jasmine didn't feel shy at all, because she had already met a lot of the female guests at the Sangeet party.

"Have you enjoyed your visit to India, Jasmine?" Priti asked as they danced.

"Yes. So much!" Jasmine said, beaming. "And I've loved getting to know you, Priti. You must come and visit me in England soon."

"Oh Jasmine, I don't know if I'll ever go to England," Priti said nervously. "I've never been on a plane before. It's scary – and what if I get travel sick?"

"Priti, you worry too much," Jasmine laughed, pulling Priti's hair loose. "You need to let your hair down."

Priti laughed and shook her hair happily as she danced. "Jasmine, you are totally right."

Things to think about

1. Why is Jasmine worried about going to her cousin's wedding? Name several things she worries about.
2. How does Priti help Jasmine to feel welcome?
3. What does Jasmine do to try and join in with the customs and traditions?
4. What happens to Dev's shoes? Why?
5. What do you think Jasmine has learnt from going to her cousin's wedding? How would you feel? Why?

Write it yourself

This story is based on experiencing something new for the first time. Think about a new place or new experience as the basis for your story.

Plan your story before you begin to write it.

Start off with a story map:

• a beginning to introduce the characters and where and when your story is set (the setting);

• a problem which the main characters will need to fix in the story;

• an ending where the problems are resolved.

Get writing! Create contrasts between the familiar and the new with descriptive words. Entice your reader with lavish details and transport them using imaginative words.

Notes for parents and carers

Independent reading

The aim of independent reading is to read this book with ease. This series is designed to provide an opportunity for your child to read for pleasure and enjoyment. These notes are written for you to help your child make the most of this book.

About the book

When Jasmine is invited to her cousin's wedding she is very excited, but also terrified. It's in Delhi, India and Jasmine has never left her local area before. She soon discovers that seeing new things and new places can be a great learning experience.

Before reading

Ask your child why they have selected this book. Look at the title and blurb together. What do they think it will be about? Do they think they will like it?

During reading

Encourage your child to read independently. If they get stuck on a longer word, remind them that they can find syllable chunks that can be sounded out from left to right. They can also read on in the sentence and think about what would make sense.

After reading

Support comprehension by talking about the story. What happened? Then help your child think about the messages in the book that go beyond the story, using the questions on the page opposite. Give your child a chance to respond to the story, asking:

Did you enjoy the story and why? Who was your favourite character? What was your favourite part? What did you expect to happen at the end?

Franklin Watts
First published in Great Britain in 2019
by The Watts Publishing Group

Series Editors: Jackie Hamley and Melanie Palmer
Series Advisors: Dr Sue Bodman and Glen Franklin
Series Designer: Peter Scoulding
Religious Consultant: Indriyesha Das, Hinduism Education Services

A CIP catalogue record for this book is
available from the British Library.

ISBN 978 1 4451 6525 7 (hbk)
ISBN 978 1 4451 6526 4 (pbk)
ISBN 978 1 4451 6943 9 (library ebook)

Printed in China

Franklin Watts
An imprint of
Hachette Children's Group
Part of The Watts Publishing Group
Carmelite House
50 Victoria Embankment
London EC4Y 0DZ

An Hachette UK Company
www.hachette.co.uk

www.franklinwatts.co.uk